AF610148

SAM DOWLING

Is a Dublin-born playwright. He has written and produced nearly thirty plays or small-cast versions of classics for Praxis Theatre Laboratory. His subject-matter has ranged from Irish history through the lives of writers and artists to re-working of themes from the Greek myths. His play about the Brontës (co-written with Andrea Bird) has had three productions in Tokyo.

For more detail see listing in playwrights' database at www.doollee.com

PRAXIS THEATRE LABORATORY is an experimental theatre which seeks its direction from the actors' response to the work. No-one takes on a separate role as director. We particularly value images conjured in rehearsal, and intuitive and emotional rather than intellectual or technical evaluation. We try to fix as little as possible and each performance retains an element of improvisation.

Founded by Sam Dowling as the in-house company at The Tabard in West London from 1984, in 1990 we left to pursue more experimental goals. We opened a small theatre space in County Roscommon, Ireland in 1999 and have toured UK, USA, Ireland, Belgium, Netherlands, Ukraine and Poland.

This small-cast version of HAMLET [for seven actors] was first performed at Boyle Arts Festival, County Roscommon in 2001, designed by Natalia Geci and with this cast;

CLAUDIUS......................Aidan Redmond

GERTRUDE..........................Maria Straw

HAMLET........................William Rowsey

OPHELIA............................Carol Brophy

LAERTES.............................Sean Duggan

HORATIO........................Olivier Schneider

POLONIUS.......................Sam Dowling

Doubling. Sean Duggan doubled as ROSENCRANTZ & GUILDENSTERN [played as one person], and PLAYERS. Aidan Redmond as GHOST, Sam Dowling as GRAVEDIGGER-CLOWN.

THE DUMB-SHOW was played by one actor using glove puppets. In the PLAY-WITHIN-THE-PLAY, the QUEEN was drawn in to play the Player-Queen.

IRISH PLAYS AND OTHERS BY SAM DOWLING
IN PRINT AT WWW.LULU.COM OR IN THE PIPELINE

RIVERMAN [Walter Greaves, naïf painter, rise and fall.]
CAULDRON OF BRONTËS [Genius siblings.]
A SEASON IN HELL [Wild poets Rimbaud and Verlaine.]
MOUNTAIN [Life-changing encounters]
RENEWAL [Site-specific version of MOUNTAIN]
TROJAN WOMEN
BIRTH OF THE BEAST [Northern Ireland.]
BIG FELLA! [Michael Collins.]
ALLEGIANCE [IRA in London.]
ANTIGONE
THE FLAME AND THE STONE [Yeats and Maud Gonne.]
VIRGIN OF NOTTING HILL [Sexual problems.]
ORESTEIAN TRILOGY
LOVELOST [Abuse]
RED COUNTESS GREEN CROW [Markievicz and O'Casey]
HA! HA! HA! [Improvisations on Coward and Shakespeare.]
CHARTISTS RISING [London 1848]

AND SMALL-CAST VERSIONS OF THESE CLASSICS;

THE CENCI
IMPORTANCE OF BEING EARNEST
CHERRY ORCHARD
THREE SISTERS
HEDDA GABLER
WHEN WE DEAD AWAKEN
HAMLET
MACBETH
ANTONY AND CLEOPATRA
THE TEMPEST

IRISH PLAYS AND OTHERS: Volume 21

Shakespeare's

HAMLET
PRINCE OF DENMARK

SMALL-CAST VERSION

BY

SAM DOWLING

e-mail praxis.lab@ntlworld.com

Published by Lulu 2008

www.lulu.com

ISBN 978-1-84799-506-3

DRAMATIS PERSONAE

CLAUDIUS, King of Denmark

GERTRUDE, Queen of Denmark, Mother to Hamlet

HAMLET, Son of the late, and Nephew to the present King

OPHELIA, Daughter to Polonius

LAERTES, her Brother

HORATIO, Friend to Hamlet

POLONIUS, Lord Chamberlain

And the following multiple roles played by DOUBLING:

FORTINBRAS [voice, off]
ROSENCRANTZ and GUILDENSTERN , COURTIER
CLOWN
PLAYERS
GHOST of Hamlet's Father

The Scene is ELSINORE

PART ONE

[HORATIO on night-watch]

HORATIO

Look how the morn in russet mantle clad
Walks o'er the dew of yon high eastern hill
Break we our watch the fearsome night is past
....
For this relief much thanks
Tis bitter cold and I am sick at heart
Now to young Hamlet for upon my life his father's ghost
Dumb to me will speak to him
I shall acquaint him with it
As needful to my love fitting my duty

[KING, QUEEN, HAMLET, POLONIUS, LAERTES.]

KING

Though yet of Hamlet our dear brother's death
The memory be green and that it us befitted
To bear our hearts in grief and our whole kingdom
To be contracted in one brow of woe
Yet so far has discretion fought with nature
That we with wisest sorrow think on him
Together with remembrance of ourselves
Therefore our sometime sister now our queen
Have we as t'were with a defeated joy
Taken to wife
The times are perilous for Denmark
Young Fortinbras of Norway
Holding a weak supposal of our worth
Sues for surrender of those lands
Lost by his father to our most valiant brother
See that the watch is kept with every vigilance

POLONIUS

Tis done my liege
By day and night

KING
And now Laertes what's the news with you ?
The head is not more native to the heart
The hand more instrumental to the mouth
Than is the throne of Denmark to thy father
What wouldst thou have Laertes ?

LAERTES
Dread my lord
Your leave and favour to return to France

KING
What says Polonius ?

POLONIUS
I do beseech you, give him leave to go

KING
Take your fair hour Laertes time be thine
And your best graces spend it as your will
And now my cousin Hamlet and my son...

HAMLET [aside]
A little more than kin and less than kind

KING
How is it that the clouds still hang on you ?

HAMLET
Not so my lord I am too much in the sun

QUEEN
Good Hamlet cast your nighted colour off
And let your eyes look like a friend to Denmark
Do not for ever with those veiled lids
Seek for your noble father in the dust
You know tis common all that live must die
Passing through nature to eternity

HAMLET
Aye madam it is common

QUEEN
If it be
Why seems it so particular with you ?

HAMLET
Seems madam ! No it is ! I know not seems
Tis not alone my inky cloak good mother
Nor customary suits of solemn black
Nor windy suspirations of forced breath
No nor the fruitful river in the eye
Nor the dejected haviour of the visage
Together with all forms modes shows of grief
That can denote me truly these indeed seem
For they are actions that a man might play
But I have that within which passes show
These but the trappings and the suits of woe

KING
Tis sweet and commendable in your nature Hamlet
To give these mourning duties to your father
But you must know your father lost a father
That father lost lost his and the survivor bound
In filial obligation for some time
To do obsequious sorrow but to persevere
In obstinate condolement is a course
Of impious stubbornness tis unmanly grief
Why should we in our peevish opposition
Take it to heart ? We pray you throw to earth
This unprevailing woe and think of us as of a father
For let the world take note
You are the most immediate to our throne
And with no less nobility of love
Than that which dearest father bears his son
Do I impart toward you

QUEEN
Let not thy mother lose her prayers Hamlet

HAMLET
I shall in all my best obey you madam

KING
That's a loving and a fair reply... Madam come
This gentle and unforced accord of Hamlet
Sits smiling to my heart
[EXEUNT all except HAMLET]

HAMLET
O ! That this too too solid flesh would melt
Thaw and resolve itself into a dew
Or that the Everlasting had not fix'd
His canon 'gainst self-slaughter ! O God ! O God !
How weary stale flat and unprofitable
Seem to me all the uses of this world
Fie on't ! O fie ! 'Tis an unweeded garden
That grows to seed...things rank and gross in nature
Possess it merely... That it should come to this
But two months dead...nay not so much not two
So excellent a king that was to this
Hyperion to a satyr...so loving to my mother
That he might not beteem the winds of heaven
Visit her face too roughly. Heaven and earth !
Must I remember ? Why she would hang on him
As if increase of appetite had grown
By what it fed on... and yet within a month...
Let me not think on it ! Frailty thy name is woman
A little month or ere those shoes were old
With which she followed my poor father's body
Like Niobe all tears why she even she...
O God ! A beast that wants discourse of reason
Would have mourned longer...married with my uncle
My father's brother but no more like my father
Than I to Hercules within a month
Ere yet the salt of most unrighteous tears

Had left the flushing in her galled eyes
She married O! most wicked speed to post
With such dexterity to incestuous sheets
It is not nor it cannot come to good
But break my heart for I must hold my tongue !
[ENTER HORATIO]

HORATIO
Hail to your lordship !

HAMLET
I'm glad to see you well Horatio
What make you from Wittenburg ?

HORATIO
A truant disposition good my lord

HAMLET
I know you are no truant
But what is your affair at Elsinore ?
We'll teach you to drink deep ere you depart

HORATIO
My lord I came to see your father's funeral

HAMLET
I pray thee do not mock me fellow-student
I think it was to see my mother's wedding

HORATIO
Indeed my lord it followed hard upon

HAMLET
Thrift thrift Horatio ! The funeral baked meats
Did coldly furnish forth the marriage tables
Would I had met my dearest foe in heaven
Ere I had ever seen that day Horatio !
My father methinks I see my father

HORATIO
O! where my lord ?

HAMLET
In my mind's eye Horatio

HORATIO
I saw him once he was a goodly king

HAMLET
He was man take him all for all
I shall not look upon his like again

HORATIO
My lord I think I saw him yesternight

HAMLET
Saw who ?

HORATIO
My lord the king your father

HAMLET
The king my father !

HORATIO
Stay till I impart this marvel to you
Two nights together on the watch
In dead vast and middle of the night
Alert for night assault by Fortinbras and Norway
Young officers were thus encountered
A figure like your father appears
Goes slow and stately by them thrice he walks
By their oppressed and fear-surprised eyes
Distilled to jelly with the act of fear
Stand dumb and speak not to him
And I with them the third night kept the watch
Where in time and form their every word made good
The apparition comes. I knew your father

These hands are not more like

HAMLET
But where was this ?

HORATIO
My lord upon the platform where we watched. I spoke to it
But answer made it none yet once I thought
It lifted up its head as if to speak
But even then the morning cock crew loud
And at the sound it shrunk in haste away
And vanished

HAMLET
Very strange

HORATIO
As I do live it's true

HAMLET
Hold you the watch tonight ?

HORATIO
I do

HAMLET
Looked he angry ?

HORATIO
More sorrow than anger

HAMLET
Pale or flushed ?

HORATIO
Very pale

HAMLET
And fixed his eyes on you ?

HORATIO
Constantly

HAMLET
I wish I'd been there

HORATIO
It would have much amazed you

HAMLET
No doubt no doubt... Stayed it long ?

HORATIO
While one with moderate haste might count a hundred

HAMLET
I'll watch tonight
Perchance twill walk again

HORATIO
I'll warrant it will

HAMLET
I'll speak to it though hell itself should gape
And bid me hold my peace so fare you well
Upon the platform I'll visit you

[EXIT HORATIO]

My father's spirit walks all is not well
I doubt some foul play would the night were come
Till then sit still my soul...foul deeds will rise
Though all the earth o'erwhelm them to men's eyes

[EXIT HAMLET .

LAERTES and OPHELIA.]

LAERTES
...And sister as the winds give benefit
And convoy is assistant do not sleep

But let me hear from you

OPHELIA
Do you doubt that ?

LAERTES
For Hamlet and the trifling of his favour
Hold it a fashion and a toy in blood
A violet in the youth of primy nature
Forward not permanent sweet not lasting
The perfume and suppliance of a minute
No more

OPHELIA
No more but so ?

LAERTES
Think it no more
For he himself is subject to his birth
He may not as unvalued persons do
Carve for himself for on his choice depends
The safety and health of the whole state
The chariest maid is prodigal enough
If she unmask her beauty to the moon
Virtue herself 'scapes not calumnious strokes
The canker galls the infants of the spring
Too oft before their buttons be disclosed
And in the morn and liquid dew of youth
Contagious blastments are most imminent
Be wary then best safety lies in fear
Youth to itself rebels though none else near

OPHELIA
I shall the effect of this good lesson keep
As watchman to my heart but good my brother
Do not as some ungracious pastors do
Show me the steep and thorny way to heaven
Whilst like a puffed and reckless libertine
Himself the primrose path of dalliance treads

And recks not his own rede

LAERTES

O fear me not
I stay too long but here my father comes

[ENTER POLONIUS.]

A double blessing is a double grace
Occasion smiles upon a second leave

POLONIUS

Yet here Laertes aboard aboard for shame !
The wind sits in the shoulder of your sail
And you are stayed for... there my blessing with thee
And these few precepts in thy memory
Look thou character. Give thy thoughts no tongue
Nor any unproportioned thought his act
Be thou familiar but by no means vulgar
The friends thou hast and their adoption tried
Grapple them to thy soul with hoops of steel
But do not dull thy palm with entertainment
Of each new-hatched unfledged comrade. Beware
Of entrance to a quarrel but being in
Bear't that th' opposed beware of thee
Give every man thine ear but few thy voice
Take each man's censure but reserve thy judgement
Costly thy habit as thy purse can buy
But not expressed in fancy...rich not gaudy
For the apparel oft proclaims the man
And they in France of the best rank and station
Are most select and generous chief in that
Neither a lender nor a borrower be
For loan oft loses both itself and friend
And borrowing dulls the edge of husbandry
This above all to thine own self be true
Thou canst not then be false to any man
Farewell my blessing season this in thee !

LAERTES

Farewell Ophelia and remember well what I have said to you

OPHELIA
'Tis in my memory locked
And you yourself shall keep the key of it

[EXIT LAERTES.]

POLONIUS
What's it Ophelia he has said to you ?

OPHELIA
Something touching the Lord Hamlet
He hath my lord of late made many tenders
Of his affection to me

POLONIUS
Affection ! pooh ! You speak like a green girl
Unsifted in such perilous circumstances think yourself a baby
That you have taken these tenders for true pay
Which are not sterling...tender yourself more dearly
I would not in plain terms from this time forth
Have you so slander any moment's leisure
As to give words or talk with the Lord Hamlet
Look to it I charge you come your ways

OPHELIA
I shall obey my lord

[EXEUNT.

HAMLET, HORATIO on the platform.]

HAMLET
What hour now ?

HORATIO
It is struck twelve draws near the season
Wherein the spirit is wont to walk

[ENTER GHOST.]

Look my lord it comes

HAMLET
Angels and ministers of grace defend us !
King father royal Dane O! answer me
Let me not burst in ignorance but tell
Why thy canonized bones hearsed in death
Have burst their cerements. Say why is this ?

HORATIO
It beckons you to go away with it. Do not go

HAMLET
It will not speak then I will follow it

HORATIO
Do not my lord

HAMLET
Why what should be the fear ?
I do not set my life at a pin's fee
And for my soul what can it do to that
Being a thing immortal in itself ?

HORATIO
You shall not go my lord

HAMLET
Unhand me Horatio
By heaven I'll make a ghost of you that stops me
I say away ! Go on I'll follow
[EXEUNT GHOST and HAMLET.]

HORATIO
He waxes desperate with imagination
To what issue will this come ?
Something is rotten in the state of Denmark
[EXIT.

GHOST and HAMLET]

GHOST

Mark me

HAMLET

I will

GHOST

My hour is almost come
When I to sulphurous and tormenting flames
Must render up myself

HAMLET

Alas ! Poor ghost

GHOST

Pity me not but lend thy serious hearing
To what I shall unfold

HAMLET

Speak I am bound to hear

GHOST

So art thou to revenge when thou shalt hear

HAMLET

What ?

GHOST

I am thy father's spirit
Doomed for a certain term to walk the night
Till the foul crimes done in my days of nature
Are burnt and purged away. List O list !
If thou didst ever thy dear father love...

HAMLET

O God !

GHOST

Revenge his foul and most unnatural murder

HAMLET
Murder !

GHOST
Murder most foul as in the best it is
But this most foul strange and unnatural

HAMLET
Haste me to know it

GHOST
Now Hamlet hear
'Twas given out that sleeping in mine orchard
A serpent stung me so the whole ear of Denmark
Is by forged process of my death
Rankly abused but know thou noble youth
The serpent that did sting thy father's life
Now wears his crown

HAMLET
O my prophetic soul !
My uncle !

GHOST
Ay that incestuous that adulterous beast
With witchcraft won to shameful lust
The will of my seeming virtuous queen
And as I slept within mine orchard did pour
Through the porches of mine ear
A leprous distilment thus was I sleeping by a brother's hand
Of life of crown of queen at once despatched
Cut off even in the blossom of my sin
No reckoning made but sent to my account
With all my imperfections on my head
But soft I scent the morning air
Adieu adieu ! Hamlet remember me

[EXIT.]

HAMLET
O all you host of heaven ! Remember thee !

Ay thou poor ghost while memory holds a seat
In this distracted globe. Remember thee !
O most pernicious woman !
O villain villain smiling damned villain !
My tables meet it as I set it down
That one may smile and smile and be a villain
At least I'm sure it may be so in Denmark

[ENTER HORATIO.]

HORATIO
Lord Hamlet ! What news my lord ?

HAMLET
O ! Wonderful

HORATIO
Good my lord tell it

HAMLET
No you will reveal it

HORATIO
Not I my lord

HAMLET
How say you then would heart of man once think it ?
But you'll be secret ?

HORATIO
Ay by heaven my lord

HAMLET
There's ne'er a villain dwelling in all Denmark
But he's a knave

HORATIO
There needs no ghost my lord come from the grave
To tell us this

HAMLET
Why right you are in the right
And so without more circumstance at all
I hold it fit that we shake hands and part
You as your business and desire shall point you
For every man hath business and desire
Such as it is and for mine own poor part
Look you I'll go pray

HORATIO
These are but wild and whirling words my lord

HAMLET
I am sorry they offend you heartily
Yes faith heartily

HORATIO
There's no offence my lord

HAMLET
Yes by St. Patrick but there is Horatio
And much offence too. Touching this vision here
It is an honest ghost that let me tell you
For your desire to know what is between us
O'ermaster't as you may. And now good friend
As you are friend scholar and soldier
Give me one poor request

HORATIO
What is it my lord ? I will

HAMLET
Never make known what you have seen to-night

HORATIO
My lord I will not

HAMLET
Nay but swear it

HORATIO
In faith my lord not I

HAMLET
Upon my heart

HORATIO
I have sworn my lord already

HAMLET
Indeed upon my heart indeed

GHOST [Beneath or OFF]
Swear

HAMLET
Ah-ha boy ! Sayest thou so ? Art thou there true-penny ?
Come on...you hear this fellow in the cellarage ?...
Consent to swear

HORATIO
Propose the oath my lord

HAMLET
Never to speak of this that you have seen
Swear by my heart

GHOST [As before]
Swear

HAMLET
Hic et ubique ? Then we'll shift our ground
Come hither friend
And lay your hand upon my heart
Never to speak of this that you have heard
Swear on my heart

GHOST [As before]
Swear

HAMLET
Well said old mole ! Canst work in the earth so fast ?
A worthy pioner ! Once more remove my friend

HORATIO
O day and night but this is wondrous strange !

HAMLET
And therefore as a stranger give it welcome
There are more things in heaven and earth Horatio
Than are dreamt of in your philosophy
But come !
Here as before never so help you mercy
How strange or odd soe'er I bear myself
As I perchance hereafter shall think meet
To put an antic disposition on
That you at such times seeing me never shall
With arms encumbered thus or this head-shake
Or by pronouncing of some doubtful phrase
As 'Well well we know' or 'We could and if we would'
Or such ambiguous giving out to note
That you know aught of me... this not to do
So grace and mercy at your most need help you
Swear

GHOST [As before]
Swear

[HORATIO swears on HAMLET's heart.]

HAMLET
Rest rest perturbed spirit. So Horatio
With all my love I do commend me to you
And what so poor a man as Hamlet is
May do to express his love and friendship to you
God willing shall not lack. Let us go in together
And still your finger on your lips I pray
The time is out of joint O cursed spite
That ever I was born to set it right

Nay come let's go in together

[EXEUNT.]

PART TWO

[POLONIUS.
Enter OPHELIA.]

OPHELIA
Alas ! my lord I have been so affrighted

POLONIUS
With what in the name of God ?

OPHELIA
My lord as I was sewing in my closet
Lord Hamlet with his doublet all unbraced
No hat upon his head his stockings fouled
Ungartered and down-gyved to his ankle
Pale as his shirt his knees knocking each other
And with a look so piteous in purport
As if he had been loosed out of hell
To speak of horrors he comes before me

POLONIUS
Mad for thy love ?

OPHELIA
My lord I do not know
But truly I do fear it

POLONIUS
What said he ?

OPHELIA
He took me by the wrist and held me hard
Then goes to the length of all his arm
And with his other hand thus o'er his brow
He falls to such perusal of my face
As he would draw it. Long stayed he so
At last a little shaking of mine arm
And thrice his head thus waving up and down

He raised a sigh so piteous and profound
That it did seem to shatter all his bulk
And end his being. That done he lets me go
And with his head over his shoulder turned
He seemed to find his way without his eyes
For out of doors he went without their help
And to the last bended their light on me

POLONIUS
Come go with me I will go seek the king
This is the very ecstasy of love
Whose violent property fordoes itself
And leads the will to desperate undertakings
As oft as any passion under heaven
That does afflict our natures. I am sorry
What ! Have you given him any hard words of late ?

OPHELIA
No my good lord but as you did command
I did repel his letters and denied
Him access to me

POLONIUS
That had made him mad
Come go we to the king
This must be known which being kept close might move
More grief to hide than hate to utter love
Come

[EXEUNT.

KING, QUEEN with
ROSENCRANTZ and GUILDENSTERN.]

ROS. & GUIL.
Both your majesties
Might by the sovereign power you have of us
Put your dread pleasures more into command
Than to entreaty
But we both obey

KING
Thanks Rosencrantz and gentle Guildenstern

QUEEN
Thanks Guildenstern and gentle Rosencrantz
And I beseech you instantly to visit
My too much changed son

ROS. & GUIL.
Heavens make our presence and our practice
Pleasant and helpful to him !

QUEEN
Ay amen !

[EXEUNT ROS. & GUIL.
ENTER POLONIUS.]

KING
What news from our brother Norway ?

POLONIUS
Good news my lord
Fortinbras is rebuked and in short
Makes vow before his uncle never more
To give assay of arms against your majesty
Whereon old Norway begs
That it might please you to give quiet pass
Through your dominions for young Fortinbras'
Commission against the Polack

KING
We'll give it gladly

POLONIUS
This business is well ended
My liege and madam to expostulate
What majesty should be what duty is
Why day is day night night and time is time
Were nothing but to waste night day and time

Therefore since brevity is the soul of wit
And tediousness the limbs and outward flourishes
I will be brief. Your noble son is mad
Mad call I it for to define true madness
What is't but to be nothing else but mad ?
But let that go

QUEEN
More matter with less art

POLONIUS
Madam I swear I use no art at all
That he is mad 'tis true 'tis true 'tis pity
And pity 'tis 'tis true a foolish figure
But farewell it for I will use no art
Mad let us grant him then and now remains
That we find out the cause of this effect
Or rather say the cause of this defect
I have a daughter have while she is mine
Who in her duty and obedience mark
Hath given me this now gather and surmise
To the celestial and my soul's idol the most beautified Ophelia...
That's an ill phrase a vile phrase ' beautified'
is a vile phrase but you shall hear. Thus...
In her excellent white bosom these &c...

QUEEN
Came this from Hamlet to her ?

POLONIUS
Good madam stay awhile I will be faithful
Doubt thou the stars are fire
Doubt that the sun doth move
Doubt truth to be a liar
But never doubt I love
O dear Ophelia ! I am ill at these numbers I
have not art to reckon my groans but that I love
thee best O most best ! believe it. Adieu.
Thine evermore most dear lady whilst this machine is to him

This in obedience hath my daughter shown me
And more above hath his solicitings
As they fell out by time by means and place
All given to mine ear

KING
But how hath she
Received his love ?

POLONIUS
What do you think of me ?

KING
As of a man faithful and honourable

POLONIUS
I would fain prove so. No I went round to work
And my young mistress I did thus bespeak
'Admit no messengers receive no tokens'
Which done she took the fruits of my advice
And he repulsed... a short tale to make...
Fell into sadness then into a fast
Thence to a watch thence into a weakness
Thence to a lightness and by this declension
Into the madness wherein now he raves
And all we wail for

KING
Do you think 'tis this ?

QUEEN
It may be very likely

POLONIUS
Hath there been such a time...I'd fain know that...
That I have positively said 'Tis so'
When it proved otherwise ?

KING
Not that I know

POLONIUS
Take this from this if this be otherwise [Head from shoulders]

KING
How may we try it further ?

POLONIUS
I'll loose my daughter to him where he walks
Be you and I behind an arras then
Mark the encounter if he love her not
And be not from his reason fallen thereon
Let me be no chamberlain
But keep a farm and carters

KING
We will try it

POLONIUS
Away ! I do beseech you both away
I'll board him presently

[EXIT KING & QUEEN.
ENTER HAMLET reading.]

O! Give me leave
How does my good Lord Hamlet ?

HAMLET
Well God-a-mercy

POLONIUS
Do you know me my lord ?

HAMLET
Excellent well you are a fishmonger

POLONIUS
Not I my lord

HAMLET
Then I would you were so honest a man

POLONIUS
Honest my lord !

HAMLET
Ay sir to be honest as this world goes is to be picked out of ten thousand

POLONIUS
That's very true my lord

HAMLET
For if the sun breed maggots in a dead dog being a good kissing carrion...
Have you a daughter ?

POLONIUS
I have my lord

HAMLET
Let her not walk in the sun conception is a blessing but as your daughter may conceive
Friend look to't

POLONIUS [Aside]
How say you to that ?
Still harping on my daughter yet he knew me not at first he said I was a fishmonger he is far gone far gone
and truly in my youth I suffered much extremity for love very near this
I'll speak to him again
What do you read my lord ?

HAMLET
Words words words

POLONIUS
What is the matter my lord ?

HAMLET
Between who ?

POLONIUS
I mean the matter that you read my lord

HAMLET
Slanders sir for the satirical rogue says here that old men have grey beards that their faces are wrinkled
their eyes purging thick amber and plumtree gum and that they have a plentiful lack of wit together with
most weak hams all which sir though I most powerfully and potently believe yet I hold it not honesty
to have it thus set down for you yourself sir could be as old as I am if like a crab you could go backward

POLONIUS [Aside]
Though this be madness yet there is method in it
Will you walk out of the air my lord ?

HAMLET
Into my grave ?

POLONIUS
Indeed that is out of the air
[Aside] How pregnant sometimes his replies are !
My honourable lord I will most humbly take my leave of you

HAMLET
You cannot sir take from me any thing that I will more willingly part withal except my life

POLONIUS
Fare you well my lord

HAMLET
These tedious old fools !

[ENTER ROSENCRANTZ and GUILDENSTERN.]

POLONIUS
There he is

[EXIT]

ROS & GUIL
God save you sir!
Mine honoured lord !

HAMLET
Most excellent good friends How dost thou Guildenstern ?
Ah Rosencrantz ! Good lads how do ye both ?

ROS & GUIL
As the indifferent children of the earth
Happy in that we are not over happy
On Fortune's cap we are not the very button

HAMLET
Nor the soles of her shoe ?

ROS & GUIL
Neither my lord

HAMLET
Then you live about her waist or in the middle of her favours?

ROS & GUIL
Faith her privates we

HAMLET
In the secret parts of Fortune ? O ! Most true she is a strumpet
What news ?

ROS & GUIL
None my lord but that the world's grown honest

HAMLET
Then is doomsday near but your news is not true
Let me question more in particular what have you my good friends deserved at the
hands of Fortune that she send you to prison here ?

ROS & GUIL
Prison my lord !

HAMLET
Denmark's a prison

ROS & GUIL
Then is the world one

HAMLET
A goodly one in which there are many confines wards and dungeons
Denmark being one of the worst

ROS & GUIL
We think not so my lord

HAMLET
Why then it is none to you for there is nothing either good or bad but thinking makes it so
to me it is a prison

ROS & GUIL
Why then your ambition makes it one tis too narrow for your mind

HAMLET
O God ! I could be bounded in a nutshell and count myself a king of infinite space
were it not that I have bad dreams

ROS & GUIL

Which dreams indeed are ambition for the very substance of the ambition is merely
the shadow of a dream

HAMLET

A dream itself is but a shadow

ROS & GUIL

Truly and I hold ambition of so airy and light a quality that it is but a shadow's shadow

HAMLET

Then are our beggars bodies and our monarchs and outstretched heroes the beggars' shadows
Shall we to the court ? for by my fay I cannot reason
Now in the beaten way of friendship what make you at Elsinore ?

ROS & GUIL

To visit you my lord no other occasion

HAMLET

Were you not sent for ? Come come deal justly with me come come nay speak

ROS & GUIL

What should we say my lord ?

HAMLET

You were sent for and there is a kind of confession in your looks which your modesties
have not craft enough to colour I know the good king and queen have sent for you

ROS & GUIL

To what end my lord ?

HAMLET

That you must teach me. But let me conjure you by the rights of our fellowship youth and love
be even and direct with me whether you were sent for or no !

ROS to GUIL

What say you ?

HAMLET

If you love me hold not off

ROS & GUIL

My lord we were sent for

HAMLET

I will tell you why so shall your secrecy to the king and queen moult no feather
I have of late... but whereof I do not know...
Lost all my mirth forgone all custom of exercises.
What a piece of work is man !
How noble in reason how infinite in faculty !
In form in moving how express and admirable !
In action how like an angel !
In apprehension how like a god ! The beauty of the world !
The paragon of animals !
And yet to me what is this quintessence of dust ?
Man delights not me no nor woman neither though by your smiling you seem to say so

ROS & GUIL

My lord there is no such stuff in my thoughts

HAMLET

Why did you laugh then when I said ' man delights not me ' ?

ROS & GUIL

To think my lord if you delight not in man what lenten entertainment the players shall receive from you

We coted them on the way and hither they are coming to offer you service

HAMLET
They shall be welcome

ROS & GUIL
There they come

HAMLET
Gentlemen your hands
You are welcome to Elsinore but my uncle-father and aunt-mother are deceived

ROS & GUIL
In what my dear lord ?

HAMLET
I am but mad north-north-west when the wind is southerly I know a hawk from a handsaw

[ENTER POLONIUS.]

POLONIUS
Well be with you gentlemen !

HAMLET
I will prophesy he comes to tell me of the players mark it
You say right sir on Monday morning it was so indeed
My good friends I'll leave you till night you are welcome to Elsinore

ROS & GUIL
Good my lord !

[EXEUNT ROS & GUIL.]

POLONIIUS
My lord I have news to tell you

HAMLET
My lord I have news to tell you. When Roscius was as actor in Rome...

POLONIUS
The actors are come hither my lord

HAMLET
Buzz buzz !

POLONIUS
Upon my honour...

HAMLET
Then came each actor on his ass...

POLONIUS
The best actors in the world either for tragedy comedy history pastoral pastoral-comical historical-pastoral tragical-historical tragical-comical-historical-pastoral scene individable or poem unlimited Seneca cannot be too heavy nor Plautus too light. For the law of writ and the liberty these are your only men

HAMLET
O Jephthah judge of Israel what a treasure hadst thou ?

POLONIUS
What a treasure had he my lord ?

HAMLET
Why
One fair daughter and no more
The which he loved passing well

POLONIUS [Aside]
Still on my daughter

HAMLET
Am I not in the right old Jephthah ?

POLONIUS

If you call me Jephthah my lord I have a daughter that I love passing well

HAMLET

Nay that follows not

POLONIUS

What follows then my Lord ?

HAMLET

Why

As by lot God wot

And then you know

It came to pass as most like it was...

The first row of the pious chanson will show you more for look where my abridgment comes

[ENTER PLAYERS.]

You are welcome welcome good friends O my old friend ! Come give us a taste of your quality

come a passionate speech

PLAYER

What speech my good lord ?

HAMLET

I heard thee speak me a speech once... twas Æneas' tale to Dido where he speaks of Priam's slaughter.

If it live in your memory

Let me see let me see...

With eyes like carbuncles the hellish Pyrrhus

Old grandsire Priam seeks

Go on....

POLONIUS

'Fore God my lord well spoken with good accent and good discretion

PLAYER

Anon he finds him

Striking too short for Greeks his antique sword

Rebellious to his arm lies where it falls
Repugnant to command....

POLONIUS
This is too long

HAMLET
Prithee say on he's for a jig or a tale of bawdry or he sleeps.
Say on come to Hecuba

PLAYER
But who O! who had seen the mobled queen....

HAMLET
'The mobled queen' ?

POLONIUS
That's good 'mobled queen' is good

PLAYER
Run barefoot up and down threatening the flames
With bisson rheum a clout upon that head
Where late the diadem stood
When she saw Pyrrhus make malicious sport
In mincing with his sword her husband's limbs
The instant burst of clamour that she made....
Unless things mortal move them not at all...
Would have made milch the burning eyes of heaven
And passion in the gods

POLONIUS
Look ! Wh'er he has not turned his colour and has tears in his eyes.
Prithee no more

HAMLET
'Tis well I'll have thee speak out the rest soon. Good my lord will you see the players well bestowed ?

POLONIIUS
My lord I will use them according to their desert

HAMLET
God's bodikins man much better use every man after his desert and who should escape whipping ?
Take them in

POLONIUS
Come sirs

HAMLET
Follow him friends we'll hear a play to-morrow
[EXIT POLONIUS.]
Old friend can you play the Murder of Gonzago ?

PLAYER
Ay my lord

HAMLET
We'll have it to-morrow
You could for a need study a speech of some dozen lines which I set down and insert in it could you not ?

PLAYER
Ay my lord

HAMLET
Very well follow that lord and look you mock him not
[EXIT PLAYERS.]
Ay so God be with ye ! Now I am alone
O! what a rogue and peasant slave am I
Is it not monstrous that this player here
But in a fiction in a dream of passion
Could force his soul so to his own conceit
That from her working all his visage wanned
Tears in his eyes distraction in his aspect
A broken voice and his whole function suiting
With forms to his conceit ? And all for nothing !

For Hecuba !
What's Hecuba to him or he to Hecuba
That he should weep for her ? What would he do
Had he the motive and the cue for passion
That I have ? He would drown the stage with tears
Confound the ignorant and amaze indeed
The very faculties of eyes and ears
I'll have these players
Play something like the murder of my father
Before mine uncle I'll observe his looks
I'll tent him to the quick if he but blench
I know my course. The spirit that I have seen
May be the devil and the devil hath power
To assume a pleasing shape yea and perhaps
Out of my weakness and my melancholy...
As he is very potent with such spirits...
Abuses me to damn me. I'll have grounds
More relative than this the play's the thing
Wherein I'll catch the conscience of the king

[EXIT.]

PART THREE

[KING, QUEEN, POLONIUS, OPHELIA,
ROSENCRANTZ & GUILDENSTERN.]

KING
And can you by no drift of circumstance
Get from him why he puts on this confusion
Grating so harshly all his days of quiet
With turbulent and dangerous lunacy ?

ROS & GUIL
He does confess he feels himself distracted
But from what cause he will by no means speak
But with a crafty madness keeps aloof
When we would bring him on to some confession
Of his true state

QUEEN
Did he receive you well ?

ROS & GUIL
Most like a gentleman
But with much forcing of his disposition
Niggard of question but of our demands
Most free in his reply

QUEEN
Did you assay him to any pastime ?

ROS & GUIL
Madam it so fell out that certain players
Are about the court and have already order
This night to play before him

POLONIUS
'Tis most true
And he beseeched me to entreat your majesties
To hear and see the matter

KING

With all my heart and it doth much content me
To hear him so inclined
So drive his purpose on to these delights

ROS & GUIL

We shall my lord

[EXEUNT ROS & GUIL.]

KING

Sweet Gertrude leave us too
For we have closely sent for Hamlet hither
That he as 'twere by accident may here
Affront Ophelia

QUEEN

I shall obey you
And for your part Ophelia I do wish
That your good beauties be the happy cause
Of Hamlet's wildness so shall I hope your virtues
Will bring him to his wonted way again
To both your honours

OPHELIA

Madam I wish it may

[EXIT QUEEN.]

POLONIUS

Ophelia walk you here. Gracious so please you
We will conceal ourselves. Read on this book
That show of such an exercise may colour
Your loneliness. We are oft to blame in this
'Tis too much proved that with devotion's visage
And pious action we do sugar o'er
The devil himself

KING [Aside]

O! 'Tis too true
How smart a lash that speech doth give my conscience !
The harlot's cheek beautied with plastering art

Is not more ugly to the thing that helps it
Than is my deed to my most painted world
O heavy burden !

POLONIUS
I hear him coming let's withdraw my lord
[EXEUNT KING and POLONIUS.

ENTER HAMLET.]

HAMLET
To be or not to be that is the question
Whether 'tis nobler in the mind to suffer
The slings and arrows of outrageous fortune
Or to take arms against a sea of troubles
And by opposing end them ? To die to sleep
No more and by a sleep to say we end
The heart-ache and the thousand natural shocks
That flesh is heir to 'tis a consummation
Devoutly to be wished. To die to sleep
To sleep perchance to dream ay there's the rub
For in that sleep of death what dreams may come
When we have shuffled off this mortal coil
Must give us pause. There's the respect
That makes calamity of so long life
For who would bear the whips and scorns of time
The oppressor's wrong the proud man's contumely
The pangs of disprized love the law's delay
The insolence of office and the spurns
That patient merit of the unworthy takes
When he himself might his quietus make
With a bare bodkin ? Who would fardels bear
To grunt and sweat under a weary life
But that the dread of something after death
The undiscovered country from whose bourn
No traveller returns puzzles the will
And rather makes us bear those ills we have
Than fly to others that we know not of ?
Thus conscience doth make cowards of us all
And thus the native hue of resolution

Is sicklied o'er with the pale cast of thought
And enterprises of great pith and moment
With this regard their currents turn awry
And lose the name of action. Soft you now !
The fair Ophelia ! Nymph in thy orisons
Be all my sins remembered

OPHELIA
Good my lord
How does your honour for this many a day ?

HAMLET
I humbly thank you well well well

OPHELIA
My lord I have remembrances of yours
That I have longed long to re-deliver
I pray you now receive them

HAMLET
No not I
I never gave you aught

OPHELIA
My honoured lord you know right well you did
And with them words of so sweet breath composed
As made the things more rich their perfume lost
Take these again for to the noble mind
Rich gifts wax poor when givers prove unkind
There my lord

HAMLET
Ha ha ! Are you honest ?

OPHELIA
My lord ?

HAMLET
Are you fair ?

OPHELIA

What means your lordship ?

HAMLET

That if you be honest and fair your honesty should admit no discourse to your beauty

OPHELIA

Could beauty my lord have better commerce than with honesty ?

HAMLET

Ay truly for the power of beauty will sooner transform honesty from what it is to a bawd than
the force of honesty can translate beauty into his likeness this was sometime a paradox but now
the time gives proof. I did love thee once

OPHELIA

In deed my lord you made me believe so

HAMLET

You should not have believed me for virtue cannot so inoculate our old stock but we shall relish of it
I loved you not

OPHELIA

I was the more deceived

HAMLET

Get thee to a nunnery why wouldst thou be a breeder of sinners ?
I am myself indifferently honest but yet I could accuse me of such things that it were better my mother had not borne me. I am very proud revengeful ambitious with more offences at my beck than I have thoughts to put them in imagination to give them shape or time to act them in. What should such fellows as I do crawling between heaven and earth ? We are arrant knaves all believe none of us. Go thy ways to a nunnery. Where's thy father ?

OPHELIA
At home my lord

HAMLET
Let the doors be shut upon him that he may play the fool nowhere but in his own house

OPHELIA
O! help him you sweet heavens !

HAMLET
If thou dost marry I'll give thee this plague for a dowry be thou chaste as ice as pure as snow thou shalt not escape calumny. Get thee to a nunnery go farewell. Or if thou wilt needs marry marry a fool for wise men know well enough what monsters you make of them. To a nunnery go and quickly too. Farewell

OPHELIA
O heavenly powers restore him !

HAMLET
I have heard of your paintings too well enough God hath given you one face and you make yourself another you jig you amble and you lisp and nickname God's creatures and make your wantonness your ignorance. Go to I'll no more on it it hath made me mad. I say we will have no more marriages those that are married already all but one shall live the rest shall keep as they are. To a nunnery go

[EXIT.]

OPHELIA
O! what a noble mind is here o'erthrown
The courtier's soldier's scholar's eye tongue sword
The expectancy and rose of the fair state
The glass of fashion and the mould of form
The observed of all observers quite quite down !
And I of ladies most deject and wretched
That sucked the honey of his music vows
Now see that noble and most sovereign reason
Like sweet bells jangled out of tune and harsh
That unmatched form and feature of blown youth

Blasted with ecstasy O! woe is me
To have seen what I have seen see what I see !

[RE-ENTER KING & POLONIUS.]

KING
Love ! His affections do not that way tend
Nor what he spake though it lacked form a little
Was not like madness. There's something in his soul
O'er which his melancholy sits on brood
And I do doubt the hatch and the disclose
Will be some danger which for to prevent
I have in quick determination
Thus set it down he shall with speed to England
For the demand of our neglected tribute
What think you on it ?

POLONIUS
It shall do well but yet do I believe
The origin and commencement of his grief
Sprung from neglected love. How now Ophelia !
We heard it all. My lord do as you please
But if you hold it fit after the play
Let his queen mother all alone entreat him
To show his griefs let her be round with him
And I'll be placed so please you in the ear
Of all their conference. If she finds him not
To England send him or confine him where
Your wisdom best shall think

KING
It shall be so
Madness in great ones must not unwatched go

[EXEUNT.

HAMLET. ENTER PLAYERS.]

HAMLET

Speak the speech I pray you as I pronounced it to you trippingly on the tongue but if you mouth it as many of your players do I had as lief the town-crier spoke my lines. Nor do not saw the air too much with your hand thus but use all gently for in the very torrent tempest and ...as I may say...whirlwind of passion you must acquire and beget a temperance that may give it smoothness

PLAYER

I warrant it your honour

HAMLET

Go make you ready

[EXEUNT PLAYERS.

ENTER POLONIUS.]

How now my lord ! Will the king hear this piece of work ?

POLONIUS

And the queen too and that presently

HAMLET

Bid the players make haste

[EXIT POLONIUS.]

What ho ! Horatio !

[ENTER HORATIO.]

HORATIO

Here sweet lord at your service

HAMLET

Horatio thou art e'en as just a man
As e'er my conversation coped withal

HORATIO

O! my dear lord...

HAMLET

Nay do not think I flatter
For what advancement may I hope from thee
That no revenue hast but thy good spirits
To feed and clothe thee ? Why should the poor be flattered ?
No let the candied tongue lick absurd pomp
And crook the pregnant hinges of the knee
Where thrift may follow fawning. Dost thou hear ?
A man that fortune's buffets and rewards
Hast ta'en with equal thanks. Give me that man
That is not passion's slave and I will wear him
In my heart's core ay in my heart of heart
As I do thee. Something enough of this.
There is a play to-night before the king
One scene of it comes near the circumstance
Which I have told thee of my father's death
Observe mine uncle if his occulted guilt
Do not itself unkennel in one speech
It is a damned ghost that we have seen
And my imaginations are as foul
As Vulcan's stithy. Give him heedful note
For I mine eyes shall rivet on his face
And after we will both our judgements join
In censure of his seeming.

HORATIO

Well my lord
If he steal aught the whilst this play is playing
And 'scape detecting I will pay the theft

HAMLET

They are coming to the play I must be idle
Get you a place

[A flourish. ENTER KING QUEEN POLONIUS
OPHELIA ROS. & GUIL. Etc.]

KING

How fares our cousin Hamlet ?

HAMLET
Excellent i' faith of the chameleon's dish I eat the air promise-crammed you cannot feed capons so

KING
I have nothing with this answer Hamlet these words are not mine

HAMLET
No nor mine now
My lord you played once in the university you say ?

POLONIUS
That I did my lord and was accounted a good actor

HAMLET
And what did you enact ?

POLONIUS
I did enact Julius Caesar I was killed in the Capitol Brutus killed me

HAMLET
It was a brute part of him to kill so capital a calf there.
Be the players ready ?

ROS & GUIL
Ay my lord they stay upon your patience

QUEEN
Come hither my good Hamlet sit by me

HAMLET
No good mother here's metal more attractive

POLONIUS
O ho ! Do you mark that ?

HAMLET [At OPHELIA's feet.]
Lady shall I lie in your lap ?

OPHELIA
No my lord

HAMLET
I mean my head upon your lap

OPHELIA
Ay my lord

HAMLET
Do you think I meant country matters ?

OPHELIA
I think nothing my lord

HAMLET
That's a fair thought to lie between maid's legs

OPHELIA
What is my lord ?

HAMLET
Nothing

OPHELIA
You are merry my lord

HAMLET
Who I ?

OPHELIA
Ay my lord

HAMLET
O God your only jig-maker. What should a man do but be merry ? For look you how cheerfully my mother looks and my father died within two hours

OPHELIA

Nay 'tis twice two months my lord

HAMLET

So long ?

O heavens ! Die two months ago and not forgotten yet ? Then there's hope a great man's memory may outlive his life half a year

[MUSIC. The dumb-show enters. A King and Queen very loving, embracing each the other. She kneels and makes a show of protest to him. He takes her up and declines his head upon her neck lays him down and she seeing him asleep leaves him. Enter a fellow takes off the crown kisses it and pours poison in the King's ears and exit. Queen returns finds King dead and makes passionate action. The Poisoner enters and seems to lament with her. He woos the Queen with gifts she seems loath and unwilling awhile but in the end accepts his love. Exeunt the dumb-show.]

OPHELIA

What means this my lord ?

HAMLET

It means mischief

OPHELIA

Belike this show imports the argument of the play

[ENTER Prologue.]

HAMLET

We shall know by this fellow the players cannot keep secrets they'll tell all

OPHELIA

You are naught you are naught . I'll mark the play

PLAYER

For us and for our tragedy

Here stooping to your clemency
We beg your hearing patiently

HAMLET
Is this a prologue or the posy of a ring ?

OPHELIA
'Tis brief my lord

HAMLET
As woman's love
Let's see the play

[BLACKOUT. The play has started .
Lights up on King and Queen.]

Player QUEEN
.... *Both here and hence pursue me lasting strife*
If once a widow ever I be wife !

HAMLET
If she should break her word !

P.KING
'Tis deeply sworn. Sweet leave me here awhile
My spirits grow dull and fain I would beguile
The tedious day with sleep

P.QUEEN
Sleep rock thy brain
And never come mischance between us twain !

HAMLET
Madam how like you this play ?

QUEEN
The lady doth protest too much

HAMLET
O! she'll keep her word

KING
Have you heard the argument ? Is there no offence in it ?

HAMLET
No no they do but jest poison in jest no offence in the world

KING
What do you call the play ?

HAMLET
The Mouse-trap. 'Tis the image of a murder done in Vienna. A knavish piece of work but what of that ? Your majesty and we that have free souls it touches us not let the galled jade wince our withers are unwrung

[ENTER PLAYER as LUCIANUS.]

This is one Lucianus nephew to the king

OPHELIA
You are a good chorus my lord

HAMLET
Begin murderer pox leave thy damnable faces. Come the croaking raven doth bellow for revenge

P. LUCIANUS
Thoughts black hands apt drugs fit and time agreeing
Confederate season else no creature seeing
Thou mixture rank of midnight weeds collected
With Hecate's ban thrice blasted thrice infected
The natural magic and dire property
On wholesome life usurp immediately

[Pours the poison into the sleeper's ears.]

HAMLET
He poisons him in the garden for his estate. His name's Gonzago the story is extant and writ in very choice Italian. You shall see how the murderer gets the love of Gonzago's wife...

OPHELIA
The king rises

HAMLET
What ! Frighted with false fire ?

QUEEN
How fares my lord ?

POLONIUS
Give o'er the play

KING
Give me some light away !

ALL
Lights lights lights !

[EXEUNT ALL except
HAMLET & HORATIO.]

HAMLET
Why let the stricken deer go weep
The hart ungalled play
For some must watch while some must sleep
So runs the world away
Would not this sir and a forest of feathers if the rest of my fortunes turn Turk with me
with two Provincial roses on my razed shoes get me a fellowship in a cry of players sir ?

HORATIO
Half a share

HAMLET
A whole one I.
For who dost know O Damon dear
This realm dismantled was
Of Jove himself and now reigns here
A very very...pajock

HORATIO
You might have rimed

HAMLET
O good Horatio ! I'll take the ghost's word for a thousand pound.
Didst perceive ?

HORATIO
Very well my lord

HAMLET
Upon the talk of the poisoning ?

HORATIO
I did very well note him

HAMLET
Ah ha ! Come some music ! Come the recorders !
For if the king like not the comedy
Why then belike he likes it not...perdy
Come come music !
[RE-ENTER ROS & GUIL.]

ROS & GUIL
Good my lord vouchsafe me a word with you

HAMLET
Sir a whole history

ROS & GUIL
The king sir...

HAMLET
Ay sir what of him ?

ROS & GUIL
Is in his retirement marvellous distempered

HAMLET
With drink sir ?

ROS & GUIL
No my lord rather with choler

HAMLET
Tell his doctor for for me to put him to his purgation would perhaps plunge him into far more choler

ROS & GUIL
The queen your mother in most great affliction of spirit hath sent me to you

HAMLET
You are welcome

ROS & GUIL
Nay good my lord...

HAMLET
My mother you say...

ROS & GUIL
Thus she says your behaviour hath struck her into amazement and admiration

HAMLET
O wonderful son that can so astonish a mother ! But is there no sequel at the heels of this mother's admiration ? Impart

ROS & GUIL
She desires to speak with you in her closet before you go to bed

HAMLET
We shall obey were she ten times our mother. Have you any further trade with us ?

ROS & GUIL
My lord you once did love me. You do bar the door upon your own liberty if you deny your griefs to your friend

HAMLET
Sir I lack advancement

ROS & GUIL
How can that be when you have the voice of the king himself for your succession in Denmark ?

HAMLET
Will you play upon this pipe ?

ROS & GUIL
My lord I cannot

HAMLET
O pray you

ROS & GUIL
Believe me I cannot

HAMLET
I do beseech thee

ROS & GUIL
I know no touch of it my lord

HAMLET
'Tis as easy as lying. Look these are the stops

ROS & GUIL
I have not the skill

HAMLET

Why look you now how unworthy a thing you make of me. You would play upon me you would seem to know my stops you would pluck out the heart of my mystery you would sound me from my lowest note to the top of my compass and there is much music excellent voice in this little organ yet cannot you make it speak. 'Sblood do you think I am easier to be played than on a pipe ? Call me what instrument you will though you can fret me you cannot play upon me

[ENTER POLONIUS.]

God bless you sir !

POLONIUS

My lord the queen would speak with you and presently

HAMLET

Do you see yonder cloud that's almost in shape of a camel ?

POLONIUS

By the mass and 'tis like a camel indeed

HAMLET

Methinks it is like a weasel

POLONIUS

It is backed like a weasel

HAMLET

Or like a whale ?

POLONIUS

Very like a whale

HAMLET

Then I will come to my mother by and by
[Aside] They fool me to the top of my bent
[Aloud] I will come by and by

POLONIUS
I will say so

HAMLET
By and by is easily said. Leave me friends
[EXEUNT ALL except HAMLET.]
'Tis now the very witching time of night
When churchyards yawn and hell itself breathes out
Contagion to this world now could I drink hot blood
And do such bitter business as the day
Would quake to look on. Soft ! Now to my mother
O heart ! Lose not thy nature let not ever
The soul of Nero enter this firm bosom
Let me be cruel not unnatural
I will speak daggers to her but use none
My tongue and soul in this be hypocrites
How in my words soever she be shent
To give them seals never my soul consent ! !
[EXIT.]

[KING, ROS & GUIL.]

KING
I like him not nor stands it safe with us
To let his madness range. Therefore prepare you
I your commission will forthwith dispatch
And he to England shall along with you
The terms of our estate may not endure
Hazard so dangerous as doth hourly grow
Out of his lunacies

ROS & GUIL
We will ourselves provide
Never alone
Did the king sigh but with a general groan

KING
Arm you I pray you to this speedy voyage

For we will fetters put upon this fear
Which now goes too free-footed

ROS & GUIL
We will haste us

[EXEUNT.
ENTER POLONIUS}

POLONIUS
My lord he's going to his mother's closet
Behind the arras I'll convey myself
I'll call upon you ere you go to bed
And tell you what I know

KING
Thanks dear lord

[EXIT POLONIUS.]

O! my offence is rank it smells to heaven
It hath the primal eldest curse upon it
A brother's murder ! What if this cursed hand
Were thicker than itself with brother's blood
Is there not rain enough in the sweet heaven
To wash it white as snow ? Whereto serves mercy
But to confront the visage of offence ?
My fault is past. But O! what form of prayer
Can serve my turn ? ' Forgive me my foul murder ' ?
That cannot be since I am still possessed
Of those effects for which I did the murder
My crown mine own ambition and my queen.
May one be pardoned and retain the offence ?
In the corrupted currents of this world
Offence's gilded hand may shove by justice
And oft 'tis seen the wicked prize itself
Buys out the law but 'tis not so above
[KING will kneel to pray.]Try what repentance can what can it not ?
Yet what can it when one can not repent ?
Bow stubborn knees and heart with strings of steel
Be soft as sinews of the new-born babe
All may be well

[ENTER HAMLET.]

HAMLET
Now might I do it pat now he is praying
And now I'll do it and so he goes to heaven
And so I am revenged. That would be scanned
A villain kills my father and for that
I his sole son do this same villain send to heaven
Why this is hire and salary not revenge
No.
Up sword and know thou a more horrid hent
When he is drunk asleep or in his rage
Or in the incestuous pleasure of his bed
At gaming or about some act
That has no relish of salvation in it
Then trip him that his heels may kick at heaven
And that his soul may be as damned and black
As hell whereto it goes. My mother stays
This physic but prolongs thy sickly days

[EXIT.]

KING
My words fly up my thoughts remain below
Words without thoughts never to heaven go

[EXIT.
QUEEN and POLONIUS.]

POLONIUS
Tell him his pranks have been too broad to bear with
And that your grace hath screened and stood between
Much heat and him. I'll silence me in here
Pray you be round with him

HAMLET [OFF]
Mother mother mother !

QUEEN
I'll warrant you
Fear me not. Withdraw I hear him coming

[POLONIUS hides

ENTER HAMLET.]

HAMLET
Now mother what's the matter ?

QUEEN
Hamlet thou hast thy father much offended

HAMLET
Mother you have my father much offended

QUEEN
Come come you answer with an idle tongue

HAMLET
Go go you question with a wicked tongue

QUEEN
Why how now Hamlet !

HAMLET
What's the matter now ?

QUEEN
Have you forgot me ?

HAMLET
No by the rood not so
You are the queen your husband's brother's wife
And...would it were not so... you are my mother

QUEEN
Nay then I'll set those to you that can speak

HAMLET
Come come and sit you down you shall not budge
You go not till I set you up a glass
Where you may see the inmost part of you

QUEEN
What wilt thou do ? Thou wilt not murder me ?
Help help ho !

POLONIUS [OFF]
What ho ! Help ! Help ! Help !

HAMLET [Draws]
How now ! a rat ? Dead for a ducat dead !
[Stabs through the arras.]

POLONIUS
O! I am slain

QUEEN
O me ! What have you done ?

HAMLET
Nay I know not is it the king ?

QUEEN
O! what a rash and bloody deed is this !

HAMLET
A bloody deed ! Almost as bad good mother
As kill a king and marry his brother

QUEEN
As kill a king !

HAMLET
Ay lady 'twas my word
[Discovers POLONIUS dead.]
Thou wretched rash intruding fool farewell
I took thee for thy better take thy fortune
Thou find'st to be too busy is some danger
Leave wringing of your hands... peace !... sit you down
And let me wring your heart for so I shall
If it be made of penetrable stuff

If damned custom have not brassed it so
That it is proof and bulwark against sense

QUEEN
What have I done that thou darest wag thy tongue
In noise so rude against me ?

HAMLET
Such an act
That blurs the grace and blush of modesty
Calls virtue hypocrite takes off the rose
From the fair forehead of an innocent love
And sets a blister there makes marriage vows
As false as dicers' oaths

QUEEN
Ay me ! What act
That roars so loud and thunders to the index ?

HAMLET
Look here upon this picture and on this
See what a grace was seated on this brow
Where every god did seem to set his seal
This was your husband look you now what follows
Here is your husband like a mildewed ear
Blasting his wholesome brother . Have you eyes ?
Could you on this fair mountain leave to feed
And batten on this moor ? Ha ! Have you eyes ?
You cannot call it love and what judgement
Would step from this to this ? O shame ! Where is thy blush ?

QUEEN
O Hamlet ! Speak no more
Thou turn'st mine eyes into my very soul
And there I see much black and grained spots
As will not leave their tinct

HAMLET
Nay but to live

In the rank sweat of an enseamed bed
Stewed in corruption honeying and making love
Over the nasty sty...

QUEEN
O! speak to me no more
These words like daggers enter in mine ears
No more sweet Hamlet !

HAMLET
A murderer and a villain
A slave that is not twentieth part the tithe
Of your precedent lord a vice of kings
A cut-purse of the empire and the rule
That from a shelf the precious diadem stole
And put it in his pocket

QUEEN
No more !

HAMLET
A king of shreds and patches...
[ENTER GHOST.]
Save me and hover o'er me with your wings
You heavenly guards ! What would your gracious figure ?

QUEEN
Alas! he's mad !

HAMLET
Do you not come your tardy son to chide
That lapsed in time and passion lets go by
The important acting of your dread command ?
O! say

GHOST
Do not forget this visitation
Is but to whet thy almost blunted purpose
But look ! Amazement on thy mother sits

O! step between her and her fighting soul
Conceit in weakest bodies strongest works
Speak to her Hamlet

HAMLET
How is it with you lady ?

QUEEN
Alas ! How is't with you
That you do bend your eye on vacancy
O gentle son whereon do you look ?

HAMLET
On him on him ! Do not look upon me
Lest with this piteous action you convert
My stern effects tears perchance for blood

QUEEN
To whom do you speak this ?

HAMLET
Do you see nothing there ?

QUEEN
Nothing at all

HAMLET
Why look you there ! Look how it steals away
My father in his habit as he lived
Look! Where he goes even now out at the portal
[EXIT GHOST.]

QUEEN
This the very coinage of your brain
This bodily creation

HAMLET
Mother for love of grace
Lay not that flattering unction to your soul
That not your trespass but my madness speaks

It will but skin and film the ulcerous place
Whiles rank corruption mining all within
Infects unseen. Confess yourself to heaven

QUEEN
O Hamlet ! Thou hast cleft my heart in twain

HAMLET
O! throw away the worser part of it
And live the purer with the other half
Good night but go not to mine uncle's bed
Assume a virtue if you have it not
Refrain to-night
And that shall lend a kind of easiness
To the next abstinence the next more easy
For use almost can change the stamp of nature
And master e'en the devil and throw him out
With wondrous potency. Once more good-night
And when you are desirous to be blessed
I'll blessing beg of you. For this same lord [Polonius]
I do repent but heaven hath pleased it so
To punish me with this and this with me
I will bestow him and will answer well
The death I gave him. So again good-night
I must be cruel only to be kind
Thus bad begins and worse remains behind
One more word good lady. You know I must to England ?

QUEEN
Alack ! I had forgot 'tis so concluded on

HAMLET
There's letters sealed and my two schoolfellows
Whom I will trust as I will adders fanged
They bear the mandate they must sweep my way
And marshal me to knavery. Let it work
For 'tis the sport to have the engineer
Hoist with his own petar and it shall go hard
But I will delve one yard below their mines

And blow them at the moon. O! 'Tis most sweet
When in one line two crafts directly meet
This man shall set me packing
I'll lug the guts into the neighbour room
Mother good-night. Indeed this counsellor
Is now most still most secret and most grave
Who was in life a foolish prating knave.
Come sir to draw towards an end with you.
Good-night mother

[EXEUNT severally.
HAMLET dragging the body of POLONIUS.

KING, QUEEN, ROS & GUIL.]

QUEEN
Bestow this place on us a little while

[EXEUNT ROS & GUIL.]

Ah ! My good lord what I have seen to-night

KING
What Gertrude ? How does Hamlet ?

QUEEN
Mad as the sea and wind when both contend
Which is the mightier. In his lawless fit
Behind the arras hearing something stir
Whips out his knife cries 'A rat ! a rat !'
And in his brainish apprehension kills
The unseen good old man

KING
O heavy deed !
It had been so with us had we been there
His liberty is full of threats to all
To you yourself to us to every one
Alas ! How shall this bloody deed be answered ?
We have loved this mad young man too much
Where is he gone ?

QUEEN
To draw apart the body he hath slain
And in his very madness he weeps for what is done

KING
O Gertrude ! Come away
The sun no sooner shall the mountains touch
But we will ship him hence and this vile deed
We must with all our majesty and skill
Both countenance and excuse. Ho ! Guildenstern !

[RE-ENTER ROS & GUIL.]

Friends both
Hamlet in madness hath Polonius slain
And from his mother's closet hath he dragged him
Go seek him out speak fair and bring the body
Into the chapel. I pray you haste in this

[EXEUNT ROS & GUIL.]

Come Gertrude come away
My soul is full of discord and dismay

[EXEUNT.

HAMLET.]

HAMLET
Safely stowed

[ENTER ROS & GUIL.]

ROS & GUIL
What have you done my lord with the body ?

HAMLET
Compounded it with dust whereto 'tis kin

ROS & GUIL
Tell us where it is that we may take it thence
And bear it to the chapel

HAMLET
Do not believe it

ROS & GUIL
Believe what ?

HAMLET
That I can keep your counsel and not mine own. Besides to be demanded of a sponge what replication should be made by the son of a king ?

ROS & GUIL
Take you me for a sponge my lord ?

HAMLET
Ay sir that soaks up the king's countenance his rewards his authorities. But such officers do the king best service in the end he keeps them like an ape in the corner of his jaw first mouthed to be last swallowed when he needs what you have gleaned it is but squeezing you and sponge you shall be dry again

ROS & GUIL
I understand you not my lord

HAMLET
I am glad of it a knavish speech sleeps in a foolish ear

ROS & GUIL
My lord you must tell us where the body is and go with us to the king

HAMLET
The body is with the king but the king is not with the body. The king is a thing...

ROS & GUIL
A thing my lord !

HAMLET
Of nothing bring me to him. Hide fox and all after

[EXEUNT.

KING attended.]

KING

How dangerous it is this man goes loose !
Yet must we not put the strong law on him
He's loved of the distracted multitude
And where 'tis so the offender's scourge is weighed
But never the offence. To bear all smooth and even
This sudden sending him away must seem
Deliberate pause diseases desperate grown
By desperate appliance are relieved or not at all

[ENTER ROS & GUIL
with HAMLET guarded]

How now ! What hath befallen ?

ROS & GUIL

Where the dead body is bestowed my lord
We cannot get from him

KING

Now Hamlet where's Polonius ?

HAMLET

At supper

KING

At supper ! Where ?

HAMLET

Not where he eats but where he is eaten a certain convocation of politic worms are e'en at him. Your worm is your only emperor for diet we fat all creatures else to fat us and we fat ourselves for maggots your fat king and your lean beggar is but variable service two dishes but to one table that's the end

KING

Alas alas !

HAMLET

A man may fish with the worm that hath eat of a king and eat of the fish that hath fed of that worm

KING

What dost thou mean by this ?

HAMLET

Nothing but to show how a king may go progress through the guts of a beggar

KING

Where is Polonius ?

HAMLET

In heaven send thither to see if your messenger find him not there seek him in the other place yourself. But indeed if you find him not within this month you shall nose him as you go up the stairs into the lobby

KING

Go seek him there

HAMLET

He will stay till you come

[EXIT someone to do so.]

KING

Hamlet this deed must send thee hence
With fiery quickness therefore prepare thyself
The bark is ready and the wind at help
The associates tend and everything is bent
For England

HAMLET

For England ?

KING

Ay Hamlet

HAMLET

Good

KING

So it is if thou knew'st our purposes

HAMLET

I see a cherub that sees them. But come for England !
Farewell dear mother

KING

Thy loving father Hamlet

HAMLET

My mother father and mother is man and wife man and wife is one flesh and so my mother. Come for England !

[EXIT.]

KING

Follow him at foot. Tempt him with speed aboard
Delay it not I'll have him hence to-night.
Away ! For everything is sealed and done
That else leans on the affair pray you make haste

[EXEUNT ROS & GUIL.]

And England if thou hold'st at aught...
As my great power may give thee sense...
Our sovereign process by sealed letters conjured
Execute the present death of Hamlet. Do it England
For like the hectic in my blood he rages
And thou must cure me. Till I know 'tis done
Howe'er my haps my joys were ne'er begun

[EXIT.

FORTINBRAS, [OFF],
at the head of his army.]

FORTINBRAS [OFF]
From Fortinbras go greet the Danish king
Tell him that by his license Norway
Claims the conveyance of a promised march
Over his kingdom

[HAMLET, ROS & GUIL.]

HAMLET
How purposed are these powers of Norway ?

ROS & GUIL
Against some part of Poland

HAMLET
Goes it against the main of Poland ?

ROS & GUIL
Truly to speak
They go to gain a little patch of ground
That hath in it no profit but the name
To pay five ducats five I would not farm it

HAMLET
Why then the Pole will ne'er defend it

ROS & GUIL
Yes 'tis already garrisoned
Will it please thee to go aboard my lord ?

HAMLET
I'll be with you straight

[EXEUNT ROS & GUIL.]

How all occasions do inform against me
And spur my dull revenge ! What is a man
If his chief good and market of his time

Be but to sleep and feed ? A beast no more
But whether it be bestial oblivion or craven scruple
Of thinking too precisely on the event
A thought which quartered hath but one part wisdom
And ever three parts coward I do not know
Why yet I live to say 'This thing's to do'
Sith I have cause and will and strength and means
To do it. Examples gross as earth exhort me
Witness this great army of such mass and charge
Led by a delicate and tender prince
Whose spirit with divine ambition puffed
Exposing all that fortune death and danger dare
Even for an egg-shell. Rightly to be great
Is to greatly find quarrel in a straw
When honour's at the stake. How stand I then
That have had a father killed a mother stained
And let all sleep while to my shame I see
The imminent death of twenty thousand men
That for a fantasy and trick of fame
Go to their graves like beds. O! from this time forth
My thoughts be bloody or be nothing worth !

[EXIT.

QUEEN and HORATIO.]

QUEEN
I will not speak with her

HORATIO
She is distract her mood will needs be pitied

QUEEN
What would she have ?

HORATIO
She speaks much of her father says she hears
There's tricks in the world and hems and beats her heart
Spurns enviously at straws speaks things in doubt
That carry but half sense her speech is nothing

Yet the unshaped use of it doth move
The hearers to collection.
'Twere good she were spoken with for she may strew
Dangerous conjectures in ill-breeding minds

QUEEN
Let her come in
To my sick soul as sin's true nature is
Each toy seems prologued to some great amiss
So full of artless jealousy is guilt
It spills itself in fearing to be spilt
[ENTER OPHELIA.]

OPHELIA
Where is the beauteous majesty of Denmark ?

QUEEN
How now Ophelia !

OPHELIA
How should I your true love know
From another one ?
By his cockle hat and staff
And his sandal shoon

QUEEN
Alas ! Sweet lady what imports this song ?

OPHELIA
Say you ? Nay pray you mark
He is dead and gone lady
He is dead and gone
At his head a grass-green turf
At his heels a stone
O ho !

QUEEN
Nay but Ophelia ...

OPHELIA

Pray you mark

While his shroud as the mountain snow...

[ENTER KING.]

QUEEN

Alas ! Look here my lord

OPHELIA

Larded with sweet flowers
Which bewept to the grave did go
With true-love showers

KING

How do you pretty lady ?

OPHELIA

Well God 'ild you ! They say the owl was a baker's daughter. Lord ! We know what we are but know not what we may be. God be at your table !

KING

Conceit upon her father

OPHELIA

Pray you let's have no words of this but when they ask you what it means say you this

To-morrow is St Valentine's day
All in the morning betime
And I a maid at your window
To be your Valentine
Then up he rose an donned his clothes
And dupped the chamber door
Let in the maid that out a maid
Never departed more

KING

Pretty Ophelia !

OPHELIA

Indeed la ! Without an oath I'll make an end on it
By Gis and by St Charity
Alack and fie for shame !
Young men will do it if they come to it
By Cock they are to blame
Quote she before you tumbled me
You promised me to wed
So would I ha' done by yonder sue
An thou hadst not come to my bed

KING

How long hath she been thus ?

OPHELIA

I hope all will be well. We must be patient but I cannot choose but weep to think they should lay him in the cold ground. My brother shall know of it and so I thank you for your good counsel. Come my coach ! Good-night ladies good-night sweet ladies goodnight good-night.

KING

Follow her close give her good watch I pray you

[EXIT OPHELIA and HORATIO.]

O! this is the poison of deep grief it springs
All from her father's death. O Gertrude Gertrude !
When sorrows come they come not in single spies
But in battalions

[A NOISE OFF]

QUEEN

Alack ! What noise is this ?

KING

Where are my Switzers ? Let them guard the door
What is the matter ?

[ENTER COURTIER.]

COURTIER

Save yourself my lord

The ocean overpeering of his list
Eats not the flats with more imperious haste
Than young Laertes in a riotous head
O'erbears your officers. The rabble call him lord
They cry ' Choose we Laertes shall be king !'
Caps hands and tongues applaud it to the clouds
'Laertes shall be king. Laertes king !'

QUEEN
O! this is counter you false Danish dogs !

KING
The doors are broke

[NOISE OFF.
ENTER LAERTES ARMED.]

LAERTES
Where is the king ? O thou vile king !
Give me my father !

QUEEN
Calmly good Laertes

LAERTES
That drop of blood that's calm proclaims me bastard
Cries cuckold to my father brands the harlot
Even here between the chaste brow
Of my true mother

KING
What is the cause Laertes
That thy rebellion looks so giant-like ?
Let him go Gertrude do not fear our person
Why art thou thus incensed ? Let him go Gertrude
Speak man

LAERTES
Where is my father ?

KING
Dead

QUEEN
But not by him

KING
Let him demand his fill

LAERTES
How came he dead ? I'll not be juggled with
Let come what comes only I'll be revenged
Most thoroughly for my father

KING
Who shall stay you ?

LAERTES
By God not all the world

KING
If you desire to know the certainty
Of your dear father's death is it writ in your revenge
That swoopstake you will draw both friend and foe
Winner and loser ?

LAERTES
None but his enemies

KING
Will you know them then ?

LAERTES
To his good friends thus wide I'll ope my arms
And like the kind life-rendering pelican
Repast them with my blood

KING
Why now you speak

Like a good child and a true gentleman

[NOISE OFF.]

LAERTES

How now ! What noise is this ?

[ENTER OPHELIA.]

O heat dry up my brains ! Tears seven times salt
Burn out the sense and virtue of mine eye !
By heaven thy madness shall be paid by weight
Till our scale turn the beam O rose of May !
Dear maid kind sister sweet Ophelia !
O heavens ! is it possible a young maid's wits
Should be as mortal as an old man's life ?

OPHELIA

They bore him barefaced on the bier
Hey non nonny nonny hey nonny
And in his grave rained many a tear...
Fare you well my dove !

LAERTES

Hadst thou thy wits and didst persuade revenge
It could not move thus

OPHELIA

You must sing a-down a-down
And you call him a-down-a
O how the wheel becomes it ! It is the false steward that stole his master's daughter

LAERTES

This nothing is more than matter

OPHELIA

There's rosemary that's for remembrance pray love remember and there is pansies that's for thoughts

LAERTES

A document in madness thoughts and remembrance fitted

OPHELIA

There's fennel for you and columbines there's rue for you and here's some for me we may call it herb of grace o' Sunday. O! you must wear your rue with a difference. There's a daisy I would give you some violets but they withered all when my father died. They say he made a good end...

For bonny sweet Robbie is all my joy

LAERTES

Thought and affliction passion hell itself
She turns to favour and to prettiness

OPHELIA

And will he not come again ?
And will he not come again ?
No no he is dead
Go to thy death-bed
He never will come again
His beard was as white as snow
All flaxen was his poll
He is gone he is gone
And we cast away moan
God ha' mercy on his soul !
And of all Christian souls I pray God God be wi' ye !

LAERTES

Do you see this O God ?

KING

Laertes go but apart
Make choice of whom your wisest friends you will
And they shall hear and judge 'twixt you and me
If by direct or by collateral hand
They find us touched we will our kingdom give
Our crown our life and all that we call ours
To you in satisfaction but if not
Be you content to lend your patience to us
And we shall jointly labour with your soul

To give it due content

LAERTES
Let this be so

KING
And so it shall
And where the offence is let the great axe fall
I pray you go with me

[EXEUNT.

ENTER HORATIO reading LETTER.]

HORATIO
Horatio, ... Ere we were two days old at sea a pirate very war-like gave us chase. Finding ourselves too slow of sail we put on a compelled valour in the grapple I boarded them on the instant they got clear of our ship so I alone became their prisoner. They have dealt with me like thieves of mercy but they knew what they did I am to do a good turn for them. Let the king have the letters I have sent and repair thou to me with as much haste as thou wouldst fly death. I have words to speak in thine ear will make thee dumb...Rosencrantz and Guildenstern hold their course for England of them I have much to tell thee. Farewell
He that thou knowest thine
Hamlet
I will give these sailors way for the letters

[EXIT.
ENTER KING and LAERTES.]

KING
Now must your conscience my acquittance seal
And you must put me in your heart as friend
For he that hath your noble father slain
Pursued my life

LAERTES
It well appears but tell me
Why you proceeded not against these feats
So crimeful and so capital

KING
O ! for two special reasons
The queen his mother
Lives almost by his looks and for myself
She's so conjunctive to my life and soul
I could not but by her. The other motive
Why to a public count I could not go
Is the great love the common people bear him

LAERTES
And so I have a noble father lost
A sister driven into desperate terms

KING
I loved your father as we love ourself
Laertes I have this letter just received from Hamlet...
High and Mighty you shall know I am set naked on your kingdom. To-morrow shall I beg leave to see your kingly eyes when I shall first asking your pardon thereunto recount the occasions of my sudden and more strange return.
Hamlet
What should this mean ?

LAERTES
Know you the hand ?

KING
'Tis Hamlet's character. 'Naked'
And in a postscript here he says 'alone'

LAERTES
Let him come
It warms the very sickness in my heart
That I shall live and tell him to his teeth
'Thus diddest thou'

KING
Will you be ruled by me ?

LAERTES
Ay my lord
So you will not o'er-rule me to a peace

KING
To thine own peace I will work him
To an explicit now ripe in my device
Under which he shall not choose but fall
And for his death no wind of blame shall breathe
But even his mother shall uncharge the practice
And call it accident

LAERTES
My lord I will be ruled
The rather if you would devise it so
That I might be the organ

KING
Two months since
Here was a gentleman of France
He made a confession of you
And gave you such a masterly report
For art and exercise in your defence
With knife and rapier most especially
This did Hamlet so envenom with his envy
That he could nothing do but wish and beg
Your sudden coming back to play with him.
Now out of this...

LAERTES
What out of this ?

KING
Laertes was your father dear to you ?

LAERTES
Why ask you this ?

KING
Hamlet is back what would you undertake
To show yourself your father's son in deed
More than in words ?

LAERTES
To cut his throat in the church

KING
No place indeed should murder sanctuarize
Revenge should have no bounds. But good Laertes
Hamlet returned shall know you are come home
We'll set a double varnish on the fame
The Frenchman gave you bring you in fine together
And wager on your heads he being remiss
Most generous and free from all contriving
Will not peruse the foils so that with ease
Or with a little shuffling you may choose
A sword unbated and in a pass of practice
Requite him for your father

LAERTES
I will do it
And for that purpose I'll anoint my blade
With mortal poison so if I scratch him slightly
It may be death

KING
Soft ! Let me see
We'll make a solemn wager on your cunnings
I have it
When in your motion you are hot and dry...
As make your bouts more violent to that end...
And that he calls for drink I'll have prepared him
A chalice for the nonce whereon but sipping
If he by chance escape your venomed stuck
Our purpose may hold there
But stay !

[ENTER QUEEN.]

How now sweet queen !

QUEEN
One woe doth tread upon another's heel
So fast they follow. Your sister's drowned Laertes

LAERTES
Drowned ! O where ?

QUEEN
There is a willow grows aslant a brook
That shows its hoar leaves in the glassy stream
There with fantastic garlands did she come
Of crow-flowers nettles daisies and long purples
That liberal shepherds give a grosser name
But our cold maids do dead men's fingers call them
There on the pendent boughs her coronet weeds
Clambering to hang an envious sliver broke
When down her weedy trophies and herself
Fell in the weeping brook. Her clothes spread wide
And mermaid-like awhile they bore her up
Which time she chanted snatches of old tunes
As one incapable of her own distress
Or like a creature native and indu'd
Unto that element but long it could not be
Till that her garments heavy with their drink
Pulled the poor wretch from her melodious lay
To muddy death

LAERTES
Alas ! Then she is drowned ?

QUEEN
Drowned drowned

LAERTES
Adieu my lord !
I have a speech of fire that fain would blaze
But that this folly douts it

[EXIT.]

KING
Let's follow Gertrude
How much I had to do to calm his rage
Now fear I this will give it start again
Therefore let's follow

[EXEUNT.

ENTER HAMLET and HORATIO.]

HAMLET
My first night at sea
In my own cabin making so bold...
My fears forgetting manners... to unseal
Their grand commission where I found Horatio
O royal knavery ! An exact command
Larded with many several sorts of reasons
Importing Denmark's health and England's too
And no not to stay the grinding of the axe
My head should be struck off

HORATIO
Is it possible ?

HAMLET
Here's the commission read it at more leisure
But wilt thou hear me how I did proceed ?

HORATIO
I beseech you

HAMLET
Being thus be-netted round with villainies I sat me down
Devised a new commission wrote it fair
An earnest conjuration from the king
As England was his faithful tributary
As peace should still her wheaten garland wear
And many a suchlike 'As'es of great charge
That on the view and knowing of these contents

He should the bearers put to sudden death
Not shriving-time allowed

HORATIO
How was this sealed ?

HAMLET
Why even that was heaven ordinant
I had my father's signet in my purse
Which was the model of that Danish seal
Next day was our sea-fight the rest you know

HORATIO
So Guildenstern and Rosencrantz go to it

HAMLET
Why man they did make love to this employment
They are not near my conscience

HORATIO
Why what a king is this !

HAMLET
Is it not perfect conscience
To quit him with this arm ?

HORATIO
It must be shortly known to him from England
What is the issue of the business there

HAMLET
It will be short the interim is mine

PART FIVE

[A Churchyard.
CLOWN digging a grave.
HAMLET and HORATIO at a distance.]

CLOWN
A pick-axe and a spade a spade
For and a shrouding sheet
O! a pit of clay for to be made
For such a guest is meet

HAMLET
I will speak to this fellow. Whose grave is this sir ?

CLOWN
Mine sir
O! a pit of clay for to be made
For such a guest is meet

HAMLET
I think it be thine indeed for thou liest in it

CLOWN
You lie out on't sir and therefore it is not yours for my part I do not lie in it and yet it is mine

HAMLET
Thou dost lie in it to be in it and say it is thine 'tis for the dead not for the quick therefore thou liest

CLOWN
'Tis a quick lie sir 'twill away again from me to you

HAMLET
What man dost thou dig it for ?

CLOWN
For no man sir

HAMLET
For what woman then

CLOWN
For none neither
One that was a woman sir but rest her soul she's dead

HAMLET
How absolute the knave is ! We must speak by the book or equivocation will undo us. How long hast thou been a grave-digger ?

CLOWN
Of all the days in the year I came to it that day that our last King Hamlet overcame Fortinbras

HAMLET
How long is that since ?

CLOWN
Cannot you tell that ? every fool can tell that it was the very day that young Hamlet was born he that is mad and sent into England

HAMLET
Ay marry why was he sent into England ?

CLOWN
Why because he was mad he shall recover his wits there or if he do not 'tis no great matter there

HAMLET
Why ?

CLOWN
'Twill not be seen in him there there the men are as mad as he

HAMLET

How long will a man lie in the earth ere he rot ?

CLOWN

Faith if he be not rotten before he die... as we have many pocky corpses now-a-days that will scarce hold the laying-in... he will last some eight year or nine year. A politician will last you nine years. Here's a skull now this skull hath lain you in the earth three and twenty years

HAMLET

Whose was it ?

CLOWN

A pestilence on him for a whoreson mad rogue ! As poured a flagon of wine on my head once. This same skull sir was Yorick's skull the king's jester

HAMLET

This ?

CROWN

Even that

HAMLET

Let me see... Alas ! Poor Yorick I knew him Horatio a fellow of infinite jest of most excellent fancy he hath borne me on his back a thousand times and now how abhorred in my imagination it is my gorge rises at it. Here hung those lips that I have kissed I know not how oft. Where be your gibes now ? Your sings ? Your flashes of merriment that were wont to set the table on a roar ? Not one now to mock your own grinning ? Quite chapfallen ? Now get thee to my lady's chamber and tell her let her paint an inch thick to this favour must she come make her laugh at that. Prithee Horatio tell me one thing

HORATIO

What's that my lord ?

HAMLET
Dost thou think Alexander looked so in the earth ?

HORATIO
Even so my lord

HAMLET
And smelt so ? Pah !
To what base uses we may return Horatio ! Why may not imagination trace the noble dust of Alexander till he find it stopping a bung-hole?
Imperious Caesar dead and turned to clay
Might stop a hole to keep the wind away
O! that this earth which kept the world in awe
Should patch a wall to expel the winter's flaw
But soft ! But soft ! Aside here comes the king

[ENTER in procession the corpse of OPHELIA, LAERTES, KING, QUEEN etc etc.]

The queen the courtiers who is that they follow ?
And with such maimed rites ? This doth betoken
The corpse they follow did with desperate hand
Fordo its own life. 'Twas of some estate
Couch we awhile and watch

[HAMLET and HORATIO retire.]

LAERTES
What ceremony else ?

PRIEST
Her obsequies have been as far enlarged
As we have warranties her death was doubtful
And but that great command o'ersways the order
She should in ground unsanctified have lodged
Till the last trumpet
For charitable prayers
Shards flints and pebbles should be thrown on her
Yet here she is allowed her virgin crants

Her maiden strewments and the bringing home of bell and burial

LAERTES
Must there no more be done ?

PRIEST
No more be done
We should profane the service of the dead
To sing a requiem and such rest to her
As to peace-parted souls

LAERTES
Lay her in the earth
And from her fair and unpolluted flesh
May violets spring ! I tell thee churlish priest
A ministering angel shall my sister be
When thou liest howling

HAMLET
What ! The fair Ophelia ?

QUEEN
Sweets to the sweet [Scattering flowers.]
I hoped thou shouldest have been my Hamlet's wife
I thought thy bride-bed to have decked sweet maid
And not have strewed thy grave

LAERTES
O! treble woe
Fall ten times treble on that cursed head
Whose wicked deed thy most ingenious sense
Deprived thee of. Hold off the earth awhile
Till I have caught her once more in my arms
[Leaps into the grave.]
Now pile your dust upon the quick and dead
Till of this flat a mountain you have maid
To over-top old Pelion or the skyish head
Of blue Olympus

HAMLET [Advances.]
What is he whose grief
Bears such an emphasis ? Whose phrase of sorrow
Conjures the wandering stars and makes them stand
Like wonder-wounded hearers ? This is I
Hamlet the Dane

[Leaps into the grave.]

LAERTES
The devil take thy soul

[They grapple.]

HAMLET
Thou prayest not well
I prithee take thy fingers from my throat
For though I am not splenetive and rash
Yet have I in me something dangerous
Which let thy wisdom fear. Away thy hand !

KING
Pluck them asunder

QUEEN
Hamlet ! Hamlet !

ALL
Gentlemen !

[They are parted and
come out of the grave.]

HAMLET
Why I will fight with him upon this theme
Until my eyelids no longer wag

QUEEN
O my son ! Upon what theme ?

HAMLET
I loved Ophelia forty thousand brothers

Could not with all their quantity of love
Make up my sum. What wilt thou do for her ?

KING
O! he is mad Laertes

QUEEN
For love of God forbear him

HAMLET
'Swounds show me what thou'lt do
Woo't weep ? Woo't fight ? Woo't fast ? Woo't tear thyself ?
Woo't drink up eisel ? Eat a crocodile ?
I'll do it. Dost thou come here to whine ?
To outface me with leaping in her grave ?
Be buried quick with her and so will I
And if thou prate of mountains let them throw
Millions of acres on us till our ground
Singeing his pate against the burning zone
Make Ossa like a wart ! Nay as thou'll mouth
I'll rant as well as thou

QUEEN
This is mere madness
And thus awhile the fit will work on him
Anon as patient as the female dove
When that her golden couplets are disclosed
His silence will sit drooping

HAMLET
Hear you sir
What is the reason that you use me thus ?
I loved you ever but it is no matter
Let Hercules himself do what he may
The cat will mew and dog will have his day

[EXIT.]

KING
I pray you good Horatio wait upon him

[EXIT HORATIO.]

[Laertes] Strengthen your patience in our last night's speech
We'll put the matter to the present push
Good Gertrude get some watch over your son
This grave shall have a living monument
An hour of quiet shortly shall we see
Till then in patience our proceeding be

[EXEUNT.

HAMLET and HORATIO.]

HORATIO

The King hath laid a great wager on your head
In combat against Laertes
Now if you are ready
You will lose this wager my lord

HAMLET

I do not think so. I shall win at the odds. But thou wouldst not think how ill all's here about my heart but it is no matter

HORATIO

If your mind dislike any thing obey it I will forestal their repair hither and say you are not fit

HAMLET

Not a whit we defy augury there's a special providence in the fall of a sparrow. If it be now 'tis not to come if it be not to come it will be now if it be not now yet it will come the readiness is all. Since no man has aught of what he leaves what is it to leave betimes.
Let be

[ENTER KING, QUEEN, LAERTES and OTHERS with foils etc etc.]

KING

Come Hamlet come and take this hand from me [The hand of Laertes.]

HAMLET

Give me your pardon sir I've done you wrong
But pardon it as you are a gentleman
This presence knows
And you must needs have heard how I am punished
With sore distraction.
His madness is poor Hamlet's enemy
Sir in this audience
Let my disclaiming from a purposed evil
Free me so far in your most generous thoughts
That I have shot my arrow o'er the house
And hurt my brother

LAERTES

I stand aloof and will no reconcilement
Till by some elder masters of known honour
I have a voice and precedent of peace
To keep my name ungored. But till that time
I do receive your offered love like love
And will not wrong it

HAMLET

I embrace it freely
And will this brother's wager frankly play
Give us the foils. Come on

LAERTES

Come one for me

HAMLET

I'll be your foil Laertes in mine ignorance
Your skill shall like a star in the darkest night
Stick fiery off indeed

LAERTES

You mock me sir

HAMLET

No by this hand

KING
Give them the foils
Cousin Hamlet you know the wager ?

HAMLET
Very well my lord
Your Grace hath laid the odds o' the weaker side

KING
I do not fear it I have seen you both
But since he is bettered we have therefore odds

LAERTES
This is too heavy let me see another

HAMLET
This likes me well. These foils have all a length ?

COURTIER
Ay my good lord

KING
Set me the stoops of wine upon that table
If Hamlet gives the first or second hit
Or quit in answer of the third exchange
Let all the battlements their ordnance fire
The king shall drink to Hamlet's better breath
And in the cup an union shall he throw
Richer than that which four successive kings
In Denmark's crown have worn. Give me the cups
And let the kettle to the trumpet speak
The trumpet to the cannoneer without
The cannons to the heavens the heavens to earth
' Now the king drinks to Hamlet !' Come begin
And you the judges bear a wary eye

HAMLET
Come on sir

LAERTES
Come my lord

[They play.]

HAMLET
One

LAERTES
No

HAMLET
Judgement

COURTIER
A hit. A very palpable hit

LAERTES
Well again

KING
Stay give me drink. Hamlet this pearl is thine
Here's to thy health. Give him the cup

HAMLET
I'll play this bout first set it aside awhile

[Trumpets & cannon.]

Come... another hit what say you ?

LAERTES
A touch a touch I do confess

KING
Our son shall win

QUEEN
He's fat and scant of breath
Here Hamlet take my napkin rub thy brows
The queen carouses to thy fortune Hamlet

HAMLET
Good madam !

KING
Gertrude do not drink

QUEEN
I will my lord I pray you pardon me

KING [Aside]
It is the poisoned cup ! It is too late

HAMLET
I dare not drink yet... madam by and by

QUEEN
Come let me wipe thy face

LAERTES
My lord I'll hit him now

KING
I do not think it

LAERTES [Aside]
And yet 'tis almost against my conscience

HAMLET
Come for the third Laertes . You do but dally
I pray you pass with your best violence
I am afeard you make a wanton of me

LAERTES
Say you so ? Come on !

COURTIER
Nothing neither way

LAERTES
Have at you now

[LAERTES wounds HAMLET then in scuffling they change rapiers and HAMLET wounds LAERTES.]

KING
Part them ! They are incensed.

HAMLET
Nay come again

[QUEEN falls.]

KING
Look to the queen there ho !

HORATIO
They bleed on both sides. How is it my lord ?

COURTIER
How is it Laertes ?

LAERTES
Why as a woodcock to my own springe
I am justly killed with mine own treachery

HAMLET
How does the queen ?

KING
She swounds to see them bleed

QUEEN
No no the drink the drink... O my dear Hamlet !
The drink the drink I am poisoned [Dies]

HAMLET
O villany ! Ho ! Let the door be locked

Treachery ! Seek it out

[LAERTES falls.]

LAERTES

It is here Hamlet. Hamlet thou art slain
No medicine in the world can do thee good
In thee there is not half an hour of life
The treacherous instrument is in thy hand
Unbared and envenomed. The foul practice
Hath turned itself on me lo! Here I lie
Never to rise again. Thy mother's poisoned
I can no more. The king the king's to blame

HAMLET

The point envenomed too !...
Then venom to thy work [Stabs the KING.]

ALL

Treason ! Treason !

KING

O ! Yet defend me friends I am but hurt

HAMLET

Here thou incestuous murderous damned Dane
Drink off this potion...is thy union here ?
Follow my mother

[KING dies.]

LAERTES

He is justly served
It is a poison tempered by himself
Exchange forgiveness with me noble Hamlet
Mine and my father's death come not upon thee
Nor thine on me ! [Dies]

HAMLET

Heaven make thee free of it ! I follow thee
I am dead Horatio. Wretched queen adieu

Thou livest report me and my cause aright
To the unsatisfied

HORATIO
Never believe it
I am more an antique Roman than a Dane
Here's yet some liquor left

HAMLET
As thou'rt a man
Give me the cup let go by heaven I'll have it
O God ! Horatio what a wounded name
Things standing thus unknown
Shall live behind me
If thou didst ever hold me in thy heart
Absent thee from felicity awhile
And in this harsh world draw breath in pain
To tell my story
The rest is silence [Dies.]

HORATIO
Now crack a noble heart. Good-night sweet prince
And flights of angels sing thee to thy rest !
...
Let me speak to the yet unknowing world
How these things came about so shall you hear
Of carnal bloody and unnatural acts
Of accidental judgements casual slaughters
Of deaths put on by cunning and forced cause
And in this upshot purposes mistook
Fallen on the inventors' heads. All this can I
Truly deliver

END

www.ingramcontent.com/pod-product-compliance
Ingram Content Group UK Ltd.
Pitfield, Milton Keynes, MK11 3LW, UK
UKHW020324250726
13967UKWH00004B/1848